A Note to Parents and Caregivers:

Read-it! Joke Books are for children who are moving ahead on the amazing road to reading. These fun books support the acquisition and extension of reading skills as well as a love of books.

Published by the same company that produces *Read-it!* Readers, these books introduce the question/answer and dialogue patterns that help children expand their thinking about language structure and book formats.

When sharing joke books with a child, read in short stretches. Pause often to talk about the meaning of the jokes. The question/answer and dialogue formats work well for this purpose and provide an opportunity to talk about the language and meaning of the jokes. Have the child turn the pages and point to the pictures and familiar words. When you read the jokes, have fun creating the voices of characters or emphasizing some important words. Be sure to reread favorite jokes.

There is no right or wrong way to share books with children. Find time to read with your child, and pass on the legacy of literacy.

Adria F. Klein, Ph.D.
Professor Emeritus
California State University
San Bernardino, California

Editor: Christianne Jones
Designer: Joe Anderson
Page Production: Melissa Kes
Art Director: Keith Griffin
Managing Editor: Catherine Neitge
The illustrations in this book were prepared digitally.

Picture Window Books
5115 Excelsior Boulevard
Suite 232
Minneapolis, MN 55416
877-845-8392
www.picturewindowbooks.com

J
793.73
Zie
Main

Printed in the United States of America.

Library of Congress Cataloging-in-Publication Data
Ziegler, Mark, 1954-
Wacky wheelies : a book of transportation jokes / written by Mark
Ziegler ; illustrated by Anne Haberstroh.
p. cm. – (Read-it! joke books–supercharged!)
ISBN 1-4048-0966-X
1. Transportation–Juvenile humor. 2. Riddles, Juvenile. I. Haberstroh,
Anne. II. Title. III. Series.

PN6231.T694Z54 2004
818'.602–dc22   2004018425

Wacky Wheelies

A Book of Transportation Jokes

By Mark Ziegler • Illustrated by Anne Haberstroh

Reading Advisers:

Adria F. Klein, Ph.D.
Professor Emeritus, California State University
San Bernardino, California

Susan Kesselring, M.A., Literacy Educator
Rosemount-Apple Valley-Eagan (Minnesota) School District

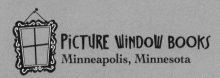

PICTURE WINDOW BOOKS
Minneapolis, Minnesota

What wobbles, flies,
and tastes good?

A Jellocopter.

Why can't a bicycle stand up by itself?

It's two tired.

What did the jack say to the car?

"Need a lift?"

What's worse than raining cats and dogs?

Hailing taxicabs.

What did one traffic light
say to the other?

*"Don't watch me while
I'm changing."*

Why did the student do her homework in an airplane?

She wanted a higher education.

What kind of trains do ballet dancers ride?

Tutu trains.

When is a car not a car?

When it turns into a garage.

What has four wheels and flies?

A garbage truck.

What do you call a
rhino on a bicycle?

Wheelie dangerous.

What do you call a duck who
flies a plane?

A flyer quacker.

Why was the airplane pilot fired?

*Because of all the days she
took off.*

What makes an airplane sick?

Flu.

What did the Boy Scout say
when he fixed the horn on
his bicycle?

"Beep repaired."

Why did the taxicab driver lose his job?

He kept driving away all his customers.

What kind of music do drivers listen to?

Car-tunes.

What should you do if your car radio doesn't work?

Get a tune-up.

What kind of car did the lobster buy for his family?

A crustacean wagon.

What kind of car does
a vampire drive?

A bloodmobile.

Why did the trucker have to visit the mechanic so often?

He was always braking his truck.

What is it called when your big brother gives you his old bike?

Re-cycling.

How is a bad car like a baby?

They both have a rattle.

What part of a car is the laziest?

The wheels. They're always tired.

Why did the man put his car in the oven?

He wanted a hot rod.

Where do cars always get a flat tire?

At the fork in the road.

What do highway troopers put on their sandwiches?

Traffic jam.

What do you call an airplane
full of elephants?

A jumbo jet.

What kind of nut is found on a rocket?

An astro-nut.

What do you call a man with a car on his head?

Jack.

What kind of truck does a road hog drive?

An 18-squealer.

What do you call a train loaded with bubble gum?

A chew-chew train.

Why did the turkey do stunts
on the skateboard?

To prove he wasn't chicken.

What do you get if you cross a dentist with a boat?

The tooth ferry.

Who invented an airplane that couldn't fly?

The Wrong brothers.

What kind of ears do trains have?

Engineers.

What do you get when you cross a chicken with a bicycle?

A hen-speed bike.

What do you call a fast tricycle?

A tot rod.

What's the best day of the week to take a plane?

Flyday.

What rabbit works at the airport?

The hare traffic controller.

How do you find a lost train?

Follow its tracks.

How did the rocket lose its job?

It got fired.

What happens to cars when they grow old?

They get re-tired.

What has 18 wheels and swims underwater?

A truck diver.

Why did the bus driver keep going around the block?

Because her turn signal got stuck.

What do you get when you cross a pig with a red light?

A stop swine.

Read-it! Joke Books— Supercharged!

Beastly Laughs: A Book of Monster Jokes by Michael Dahl

Chalkboard Chuckles: A Book of Classroom Jokes by Mark Moore

Creepy Crawlers: A Book of Bug Jokes by Mark Moore

Critter Jitters: A Book of Animal Jokes by Mark Ziegler

Giggle Bubbles: A Book of Underwater Jokes by Mark Ziegler

Goofballs! A Book of Sports Jokes by Mark Ziegler

Lunchbox Laughs: A Book of Food Jokes by Mark Ziegler

Roaring with Laughter: A Book of Animal Jokes by Michael Dahl

School Kidders: A Book of School Jokes by Mark Ziegler

Sit! Stay! Laugh! A Book of Pet Jokes by Michael Dahl

Spooky Sillies: A Book of Ghost Jokes by Mark Moore

Wacky Wheelies: A Book of Transportation Jokes by Mark Ziegler

Looking for a specific title or level? A complete list of *Read-it!* Readers is available on our Web site: *www.picturewindowbooks.com*